Cape Charles

A to Z

by Katie Hines Porterfield

Art by Julia Bridgforth

www.mascotbooks.com

Cape Charles A to Z

Art by Julia Bridgforth
Book Design by Julia Bridgforth and Circa Design

For more information, please contact:
Mascot Books
620 Herndon Parkway #320
Herndon, VA 20170
info@mascotbooks.com

Library of Congress Control Number: 2019915452

CPSIA Code: PRT1119A
ISBN-13: 978-1-64543-339-2

Printed in the United States

For all the children who call Cape Charles home.

-Katie

To the Bridgforth clan,
May we always return to the Shore.

-Julia

On the southern tip of Virginia's Eastern Shore,
there's a special place you must explore.
Cape Charles, they call it, Virginia's own Cape,
an old railroad town that's become an escape.
You'll find it when you head up Route 13,
through the longest bridge-tunnel I've ever seen.
It's perched between the Atlantic and the Chesapeake Bay,
on the Delmarva Peninsula, they like to say.
Many own houses or live here like me,
but others stay in a hotel or a B&B.
Cape Charles is quaint and the pace is slow.
There's so much fun to be had here, though.
So, join me and I'll show you all there is to do and see.
We'll take a little tour, as I fly from A to Z.

Kick off summer with
Art and Music on the Farm.

The **B**each is part of the Cape Charles charm.

That Candy Company fudge is delicious, I'm told.

Historic District homes are more than 100 years old.

The Shanty is a famous Eatery with a view.

Fish from the pier or watch while others do.

Head to Bay Creek
to hit a **G**olf ball.

The **H**arbor is where watermen offload their haul.

Ice cream and shave Ice taste good in the sun.

Fourth of July weekend is tons of fun.

Kiptopeke is a nice spot to hike or camp out.

The **LOVE** sign is what Cape Charles is all about.

Wander **M**ason Avenue for art galleries and cute shops.

The **N**atural Area Preserve is one of my favorite stops.

The festival at the Oyster Farm
is pretty neat.

Visit Peach Street Books for
a good read or a treat.

Enjoy some **Quiet** as the sun begins to set.

Have you tried the breakfast at **R**ayfield's yet?

Hop on a tall **S**hip
and perhaps take a ride.

Fill a bucket with
hermit crabs at low **T**ide.

Underwater there are creatures galore.

The Farmers' Market
has **V**eggies and more.

The **W**ater Tower will help you find the way.

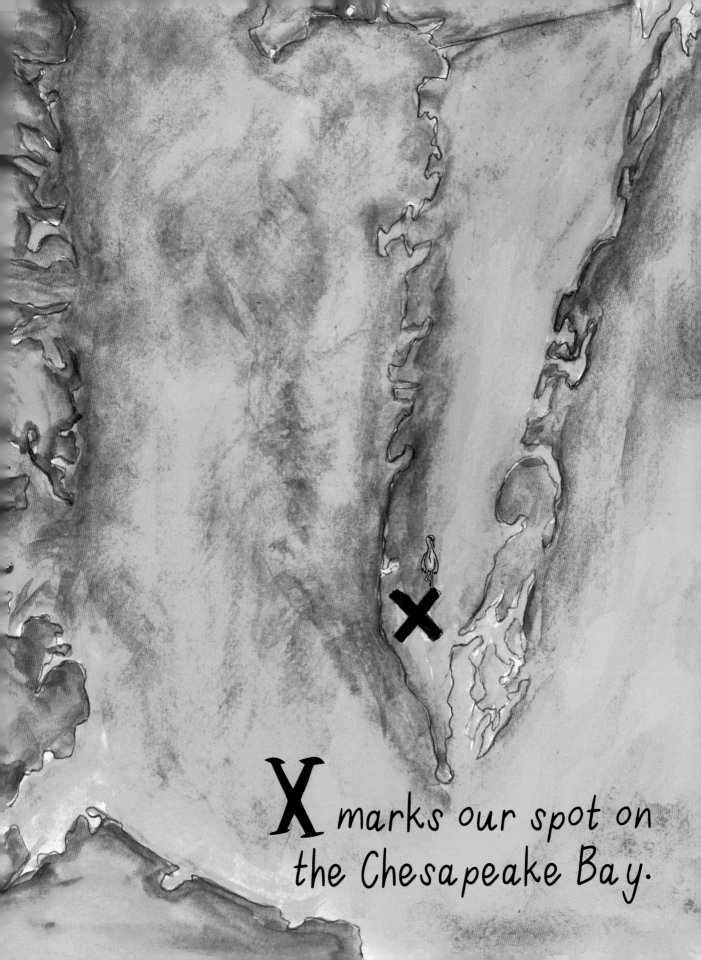

X marks our spot on the Chesapeake Bay.

Yay, there's a band at Central Park!

Let's catch some **ZZZ**s
—it's really dark!

AUTHOR

Katie Hines Porterfield

A writer based in Nashville, Tennessee, Katie Hines Porterfield created A to Z Children's Books to capture what folks love about places that make them happy. She relies on talented artists with a connection to each locale to bring her words to life, giving each book a style that's as unique as the place itself. Her growing brand of books includes *Sewanee A to Z, Find Your Heart in Lake Martin: An A to Z Book, The Homestead A to Z, Smith Lake A to Z* and *The Sewanee Night Before Christmas.* Katie holds a B.A. in American Studies from the University of The South and an M.A. in journalism from the University of Alabama. She and her husband, Forrest, are the parents of twin boys, Hines and Shep, who serve as the most honest and discerning editors and amaze, challenge, and inspire her on a daily basis. Purchase her books at atozchildrensbooks.com and follow her on Instagram and Facebook @atozchildrensbooks.

ARTIST

Julia Bridgforth

Cape Charles native and nature lover Julia Bridgforth is on a mission to tell stories of meaningful people, places, and organizations through art and illustration. After receiving a B.A. in Environmental Arts and Humanities from the University of the South, she skipped over to Vanderbilt in Nashville, Tennessee, to complete a Masters of Marketing degree. Growing up in Cape Charles, Julia spent her fair share of time kayaking the salt marshes, dancing at Art and Music on the Farm, collecting hermit crabs at the beach, and even served at both Brown Dog Ice Cream and The Shanty! Her love of the town grows every day.